SABOTAGE

MARS BOUND

TRACY WOLFF

ILLUSTRATED BY PAT KINSELLA

Spellbound

An Imprint of Magic Wagon
abdopublishing.com

FOR NOOR, YOU REALLY ARE THE LIGHT OF MY LIFE. —TW

abdopublishing.com

Published by Magic Wagon, a division of ABDO, PO Box 398166, Minneapolis,
Minnesota 55439. Copyright © 2017 by Abdo Consulting Group, Inc. International
copyrights reserved in all countries. No part of this book may be reproduced in any
form without written permission from the publisher. Spellbound™ is a trademark
and logo of Magic Wagon.

Printed in the United States of America, North Mankato, Minnesota.
092016
012017

Written by Tracy Wolff
Illustrated by Pat Kinsella
Edited by Tamara L. Britton
Designed by Laura Mitchell

Publisher's Cataloging-in-Publication Data

Names: Wolff, Tracy, author. | Kinsella, Pat, illustrator.
Title: Sabotage / by Tracy Wolff ; illustrated by Pat Kinsella.
Description: Minneapolis, MN : Magic Wagon, 2017. | Series: Mars bound ; Book 2
Summary: Braden Green, Gabriel Lopez and Misty Everest discover the damage
    to the spaceship is the result of sabotage, and they must figure out who is
    behind it before something else goes wrong.
Identifiers: LCCN 2016948527 | ISBN 9781624021985 (lib. bdg.) |
    ISBN 9781624022586 (ebook) | ISBN 9781624022883 (Read-to-me ebook)
Subjects: LCSH: Mars (Planet)--Juvenile fiction. | Survival--Juvenile fiction. |
    Space ships--Juvenile fiction. | Adventure and adventurers--Juvenile
    fiction.
Classification: DDC [Fic]--dc23
LC record available at http://lccn.loc.gov/2016948527

J
Wolff

TABLE OF
CONTENTS

ONE
ALONE

In the ship's command center,
the captain is *dead*. So is the rest
of the crew—all of the adults.
They're all *dead*. Victims of
what the captain told us was a
MALFUNCTION
that breached the spaceship's hull.

To keep the ship pressurized, we
SEALED off the compromised
sections. But it's only temporary.

HURTLING through space

at 24,000 miles per hour will only cause

more DAMAGE to the ship.

I'm trying not to **PANIC**.

Braden and Misty are doing the

same. But it isn't *easy*.

We're on a spaceship bound

for **MARS**. And according to the

computer data in front of us, the ship

is **drifting** off course.

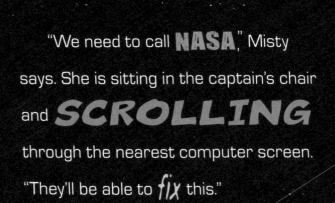

"We need to call **NASA**," Misty says. She is sitting in the captain's chair and *SCROLLING* through the nearest computer screen. "They'll be able to *fix* this."

We're **ALONE** on the bridge.

Well, alone except for the bodies of the crew. We **SHOVED** them to the floor and covered them with silver space blankets from the **EMERGENCY** kits.

"What can **NASA** do?" Braden

DEMANDS "We're a

hundred million miles away from them!"

"**NASA** can control the *Wanderer*

from Earth," I remind him. "They could

program a course correction."

Braden *shakes* his head. "If they could get us back on **COURSE**, don't you think they would have done it already?"

12

"Maybe they don't know anything is **WRONG** yet," Misty says. "Are they sleeping? Are they on vacation? Did they suddenly forget that we're up here traveling to **MARS**?"

I get Braden's point. Manned SPACE travel to Mars has become more common in the last fifty years. But it's still not normal. NASA closely MONITORS every ship it sends to Mars. Especially since the fate of EARTH depends on the continued success of the colony.

"If NASA isn't taking remote control of the ship or communicating with us, it's because they can't," I say. "We're on our own."

TWO
CONUNDRUM

"So what do we do?" Misty asks. "If we **drift** too far off COURSE, we'll miss MARS completely."

"We need to find out if there's anyone still alive on the SHIP who can do a COURSE correction," I say as I settle into the co-captain's chair. I try not to LOOK at his blanket-covered body on the ground near my feet.

"We'll have to do that without causing a **PANIC**," Braden says.

He paces between the ship's front **WINDOWS** and the captain's station.

"We don't need everyone on board
FREAKING out."

Braden sits down in the chair and *swipes* the computer screen. He's looking for something that explains how to get the **WANDERER** on course.

But before he can do more than click an icon, the ship **STUTTERS** like a kid who *TRIPPED* over his own feet. I *JOLT* forward, my body slamming against the console in front of me.

Misty and Braden are on the floor. None of us can move because of a **RAPID** deceleration. I struggle to turn my head and look at the screen that displays our speed. We've **DROPPED** 8,000 miles per hour and the number is still *falling*. If we stop completely, it will take a long time to get the constant *ACCELERATION* engine back up to speed.

SCREAMS echo throughout the ship as the rest of the passengers grow more *frantic.*

"This doesn't make sense," Braden says. "MALFUNCTIONS don't work like this."

"Then what's causing this?" I DEMAND.

THREE

COMPLICATION

"Not what," Braden answers grimly.

"Who. And we need to find them before

they **DESTROY** the whole ship."

"How are we going to do that?" I ask.

"We can't even **MOVE!**"

"We have to try," he answers.

He's right. If someone is doing this,

then we have to **STOP** them before they

cause **DAMAGE** that can't be *fixed*. I try

not to think that maybe they already have.

Slowly, *Painfully,*

I reach for the computer screen closest

to me. I scroll to the home page and

search for an icon I saw earlier.

When I find it, I swipe my finger

across it and the `artificial` gravity

screen **pops** up.

I *slide* the SWITCH to off,

and seconds later I can MOVE again.

The artificial gravity makes it possible to walk around the SHIP like we are still on Earth. Without it, we don't feel the DECELERATION the same way.

But now we're all **floating**. I scroll to the **intercom** switch Misty used earlier and then **grab** hold of the microphone.

"This is Officer Gabriel Lopez. This loss of **gravity** is temporary," I tell the frightened passengers. "We'll SWITCH it back on as soon as we can. The crew is working to get the **LIGHTS** back on. In the meantime, hang TIGHT."

I *TURN* off the microphone and then SOMERSAULT to face my friends. "Where do we start?"

"The only place besides the bridge where someone could do this much **DAMAGE**," Misty says.

"The engine room."

FOUR
CULPRIT

We *propel* ourselves toward the door. Then Braden **STOPS** and takes something from one of the bodies now floating around the room.

"What are you doing?" I ask.

"We might need a weapon," he says, holding up a STUNNER.

I don't like the sound of that, but he's right. "Get one for Misty and me, too."

I shine my FLASHLIGHT as we float through NARROW hallways to the engine room. It's way on the other side of the ship. The DARKNESS is made eerie by cries and screams that ECHO through the ship. I'm scared of what we'll find and of what will happen to us.

We finally get to the **engine**

room and listen at the door. Someone is

MOVING around inside.

"What do we do?" I *whisper*

to Braden.

He holds up his

STUNNER.

After a second, Misty and I do

the same. Then I turn off the

FLASHLIGHT.

We go in LOW, in case the person inside has a weapon. The movement STOPS. But I can hear someone breathing in the corner of the room.

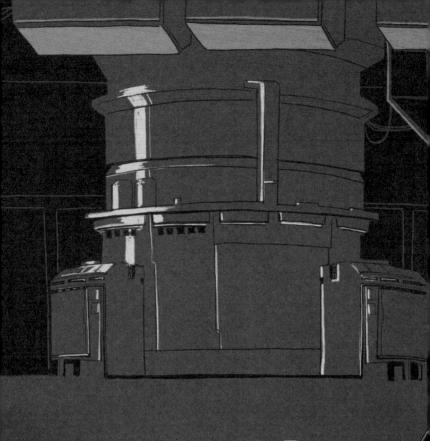

I *NUDGE*

Braden and point. We move

toward the **SOUND**.

But Misty *beats* us to it. She flips

her flashlight on and **SHINES**

it into the **trespasser's** eyes.

I recognize him as Alex Rask, one of

the guys from my training group. He'd

FOUGHT against

coming to Mars. But in the end, he

had no choice. Just like the rest of us.

"Don't move," Braden says, his **STUNNER** at the ready. Alex ignores him and tries to duck down behind one of the engine's big **cooling** pods.

Braden fires and Alex's body **convulses**, then goes *limp.*

He floats, unconscious, in front of us.

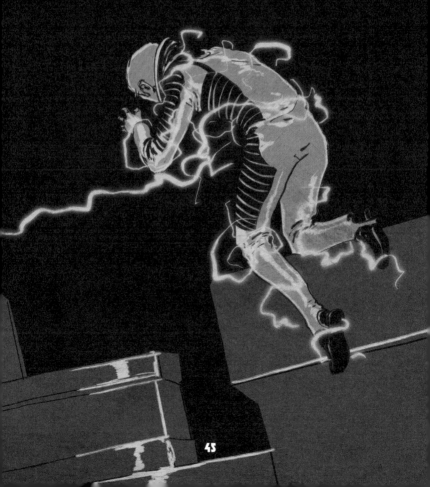

"We need to figure out what he did," Misty tells us even as she starts looking over the **engine** for DAMAGE. "And hope we can *fix* it."

"We can *fix* it," I say as I find rope. I *bind* Alex's hands and feet and then tie him to the nearest **SUPPORT** beam.

"How do you know?" she asks.

"Because we don't have a choice," Braden says, *turning* on his **FLASHLIGHT.**

"Now, let's get to work."